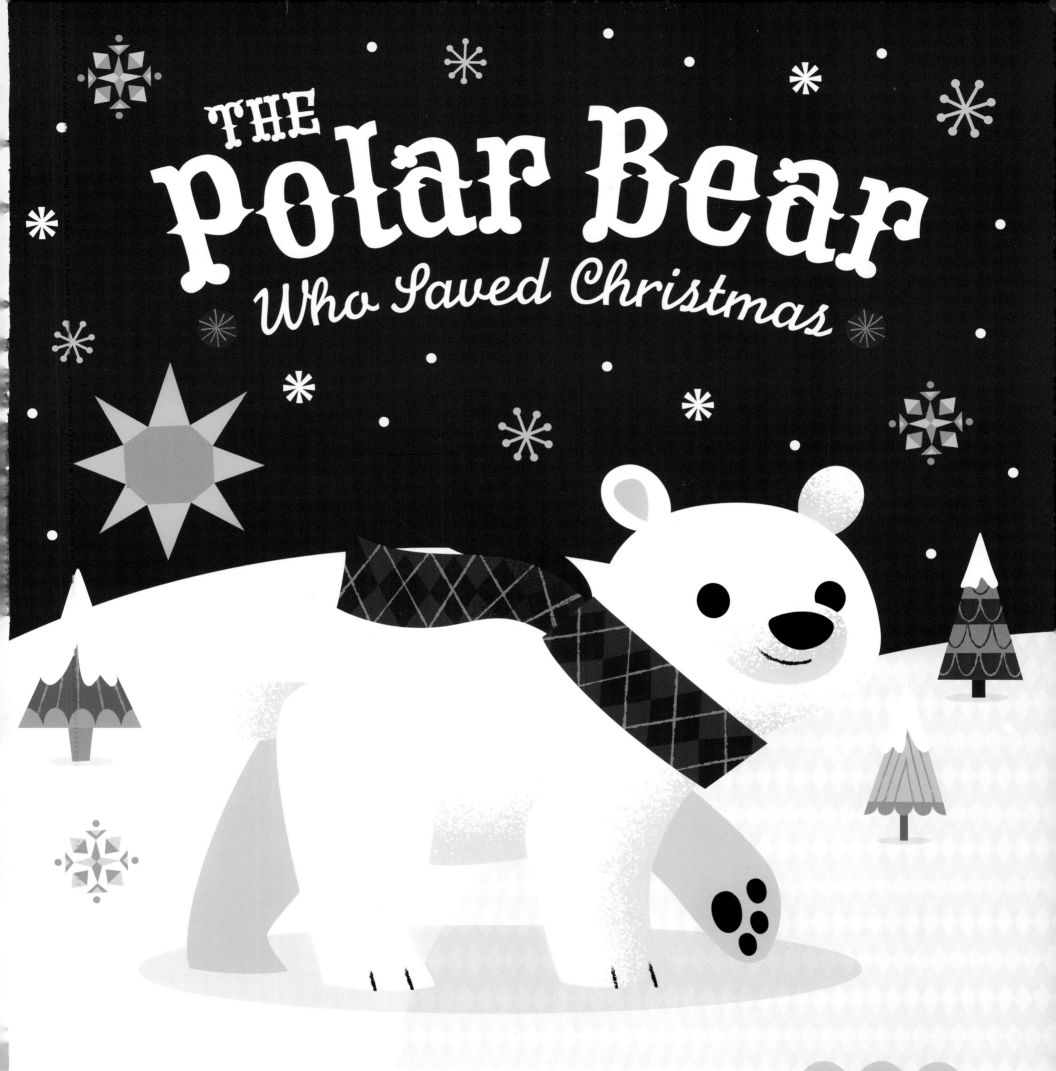

# THE Polar Bear
## Who Saved Christmas

Written by Fiona Boon

Copyright © 2021
**make believe ideas ltd**
The Wilderness, Berkhamsted, Hertfordshire, HP4 2AZ, UK.
557 Broadway, New York, NY 10012, USA.

One *Christmas Eve,* in a den in the snow,
a ***polar bear*** slept and so didn't know
that her CUB was awake. *Pip* could not rest –

Z
Z
Z

he was excited for Christmas,
the day he *loved* best!

In the distance, *Pip* heard a *jingling* sound.
He jumped up and popped his head above ground.

POLAR
BEAR
HOME

Pressed in the snow,

he saw **tracks** lead away.

He said to himself,

"It **must** be a *sleigh!*"

Pip walked through the snow
'til the jingling was gone.
Alone in the cold,
he soon missed his mom.
Fresh snow hid his paw prints
and covered the tracks.

With **no** path to follow,

would he **find** his way back?

But then the snow stopped,
and a blaze of bright light
led Pip to a strange and *magical* sight.

There were warm, cozy houses
and *elves* everywhere –
*hope* lifted the heart of the cold *polar bear!*

Pip peered through a window

as he heard a loud wail:

"Dancer's broken her leg!
Who'll take Santa's mail?"

Inside was a sleigh filled with fine toys and treats.
Nearby, an elf shouted
and stamped
her small feet.

December

The **reindeer** were worried –
they felt at a loss!
The elf looked around
and said (getting cross),

"We have seven **reindeer**,
but our **sleigh** needs eight.
If we wait for Dancer,
it will be too late!"

As they pulled out the **sleigh**,

the elves made a **fuss** –

what could they do to **save** this

**Christmas?**

An elf soon saw **Pip** and said,
"Don't be shy!
Can you pull the **sleigh?**"

But **Pip** said,
"I can't **fly!**"

The elves said, "Don't worry!"
and put **Pip** in line.

"With your *help*,
we'll certainly make it in time."

They sprinkled some *sparkles* and *Pip* gave a sneeze!

He felt **brave** and knew it was now **time** to leave.

Santa jumped on
and took hold of the reins.
The *reindeer* leapt forward,
so *Pip* did the *same*.

The earth fell away as the huge *sleigh* took flight . . .

and *Pip* and the *reindeer* flew off into the night.

They leapt across rooftops, delivering *toys*
to the **homes** of all the young girls and boys.

In bed, sound asleep,

no child was aware

that *Santa's* new helper

was a small *polar bear!*

Pip and the reindeer worked hard through the night,
delivering joy on their magical flight.

The sleigh headed home when each *gift* was gone.

And though *Pip* was tired, they all CHEERED him on.

Then **Pip** saw his **den** —
such a ***wonderful*** sight!

He **slipped** from the reins
and took **one** final ***flight.***

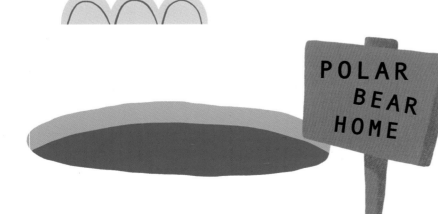

POLAR
BEAR
HOME

Cozy and *warm*

in the snow so deep,

curled up in his bed,

*Pip* fell straight asleep.

Early the next morning,
no tracks could be seen.
Pip looked around —

had it all been a **dream?**

But in the **snow** lay a **note**
and a ***shiny*** sleigh bell,

"For the ***bear*** who saved *Christmas,*
*Santa* wishes you well."